The Ladybird Key Words Reading Scheme is based on these commonly used words. Those used most often in the English language are introduced first—with other words of popular appeal to children. All the Key Words list is covered in the early books, and the later titles use further word lists to develop full reading fluency. The total number of different words which will be learned in the complete reading scheme is nearly two thousand. The gradual introduction of these words, frequent repetition and complete 'carry-over' from book to book, will ensure rapid learning.

The full colour illustrations have been designed to create a desirable attitude towards learning—by making every child *eager* to read each title. Thus this attractive reading scheme embraces not only the latest findings in word frequency, but also the natural interests and activities of happy children.

Each book contains a list of the new words introduced.

W MURRAY, the
Reading Scheme, i
and lecturer on the
with J McNally, of
book published by 7

THE LADYBIRD KEY WORDS READING SCHEME has 12 graded books in each of its three series—'a', 'b' and 'c'. These 36 graded books are all written on a controlled vocabulary, and take the learner from the earliest stages of reading to reading fluency.

The 'a' series gradually introduces and repeats new words. The parallel 'b' series gives the needed further repetition of these words at each stage, but in a different context and with different illustrations.

The 'c' series is also parallel to the 'a' series, and supplies the necessary link with writing and phonic training.

An illustrated booklet—*Notes for using the Ladybird Key Words Reading Scheme*—can be obtained free from the publishers. This booklet fully explains the Key Words principle. It also includes information on the reading books, work books and apparatus available, and such details as the vocabulary loading and reading ages of all books.

Published by Ladybird Books Ltd Loughborough Leicestershire UK
Ladybird Books Inc Auburn Maine 04210 USA
© LADYBIRD BOOKS LTD MCMLXIV
All rights reserved. No part of this publication may be reproduced, stored in a retrieval system, or transmitted in any form or by any means, electronic, mechanical, photo-copying, recording or otherwise, without the prior consent of the copyright owner.
Printed in England

BOOK 3b
The Ladybird Key Words Reading Scheme

Boys and girls

by W. MURRAY
with illustrations by MARTIN AITCHISON

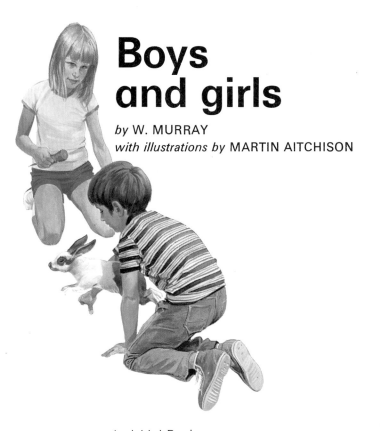

Ladybird Books

Peter and Jane are
at home.

They are at play.

Look at this, says Peter.

We like to jump.

We can jump on this.

We can have some fun
on this.

---

at   play   on

Peter and Jane like to play.

I want to jump on this, says Peter.

Look at me, Jane.

Look at me.

Up I go.

Up and up I go.

It's fun to play on this.

---

me Up up

Jane wants to play.

I want to play, please,
Jane says.

Peter, I want to jump,
please.

Jane jumps up and down.

Up and down I go,
Jane says.

Up and down, up and
down.

Look at me, Peter.

---

please   down

Peter likes to help.

He sees Daddy go up.

He wants to help Daddy.

I want to help you,
he says.

Please can I help you?

Yes, says Daddy, you can
help me.

---

help   sees   Daddy

Here comes Jane with some tea.

This is for you, Daddy, Jane says.

Here you are. Here's some tea for you. Come down for the tea, please.

Daddy sees Jane with the tea, and comes down.

---

with   tea

Here's Daddy with some apples.

Peter has an apple, and Jane has an apple.

Peter and Jane see Daddy go up and down.

They want to help Daddy with the apples.

---

an   apple   apples

Peter and Jane are in the car with Daddy.

They like it in the car.

Mummy is at home.

They see a toy shop and a sweet shop.

Peter wants to see the school.

car   Mummy   school

They go on to the school.

Here it is, says Peter,
here's the school.

Peter and Jane like the
school.

Here's a cake shop,
says Daddy.

Mummy wants some cakes.

We have to get cakes
for tea.

cake   cakes   get

Here we are at home,
says Daddy.

Peter helps Daddy with
the car, and Jane helps
Mummy get the tea.

Good girl, says Mummy
to Jane.

You are a good girl to
help me like this.

Good   good   girl

Jane and Peter like to play with the rabbits.

Peter has one, and Jane has one.

They are good to the rabbits.

Peter's rabbit can jump, and Jane's rabbit can jump.

The rabbits like Peter and Jane.

---

rabbit   rabbits   one

Here's a home for the rabbits.

Daddy helps Peter with it, and the dog looks on.

It's Pat. He's a good dog.

Pat likes rabbits.

He likes to play with the rabbits.

Peter and Jane have some flowers.

Jane says, Girls like flowers.

Peter says, Yes, and boys like flowers.

Jane wants to have a flower shop.

Peter helps with it.

He gets some red flowers for Jane.

---

flowers   boys   red

Here's a tree, says Jane,
and here are some
flowers.

Come and look, Peter.

Look at the red flowers
and the tree.

Peter looks.

Yes, he says, I like the tree
and I like the flowers.

This is a boat, says Peter, a boat on the water.

Here's a man in a boat.

A boy is with the man.

Have a look, Jane.

Have a look at this red boat on the water.

---

boat   man

I want a boat, says Peter.

I want one to play with.

Please help me, Daddy.

Please help me with this.

I want some help with this.

Yes, says Daddy, I want to
help you with the boat.

Here's Peter with the boat.

It's a red one.

He wants to go to the water with the boat.

Daddy gets the car to go to the water.

Jane is in the car.

Here they are, at the water.

Peter is in the water with the red boat.

He has fun in the water with the boat.

Can you see a fish in the water? says Jane.

No, says Peter.

Peter sees a man and a boy.

The man has a boat.

It's a Police boat.

Peter says to Jane,
Look at that boat.

That man has a Police boat.

I like that Police boat.

Police   that

This is the school.

The boys and girls are at school.

Here are the Police.

The Police are at the school.

They have come in a Police car.

They have come to help the boys and girls.

Peter has a toy car.

Jane is with Peter.

Jane says, Here's a shop with apples.

Please get some apples, Peter.

Go into this shop for some apples.

Yes, we want some apples, says Peter.

Peter and Jane want to go
to the station to see
the trains.

They like to look at the
trains at the station.

Here they go, on a bus
to the station.

It's a red bus.

They like it on the bus.

---

station   train   trains   bus

The bus has come to the station.

Peter and Jane go into the station.

They like to see the trains.

I like to go on a train with Mummy and Daddy, says Jane.

Yes, it's fun to go on a train, says Peter.

The boy and the girl are at home.

It was fun at the station, says Jane.

Yes, it was fun to see the trains, says Peter.

He gives a ball to Pat.

Mummy gives Peter an apple, and gives some cakes to Jane.

---

was   gives

The toys go in here,
says Jane.

Mummy says, You have
to go to bed, Jane.

You have to go to bed,
Peter.

Come on, up to bed
you go.

You are a good girl, Jane,
and you are a good
boy, Peter.

---

bed

New words used in this book

Total number of new words 36

The vocabulary of this book is the same
as that of the parallel reader 3a.